W9-AUR-050

Nick and Nack
Put on a Puppet Show

By Brandon Budzi
Art by Adam Record

HIGHLIGHTS PRESS

Honesdale, Pennsylvania

Stories + Puzzles = Reading Success!

Dear Parents,

Highlights Puzzle Readers are an innovative approach to learning to read that combines puzzles and stories to build motivated, confident readers.

Developed in collaboration with reading experts, the stories and puzzles are seamlessly integrated so that readers are encouraged to read the story, solve the puzzles, and then read the story again. This helps increase vocabulary and reading fluency and creates a satisfying reading experience for any kind of learner. In addition, solving Hidden Pictures puzzles fosters important reading and learning skills such as:

- shape and letter recognition
- letter-sound relationships
- visual discrimination
- logic
- flexible thinking
- sequencing

With high-interest stories, humorous characters, and trademark puzzles, Highlights Puzzle Readers offer a winning combination for inspiring young learners to love reading.

This
is Nick.

This is
Nack.

Nick loves to **make** things.
Nack loves to **find** things.
They make a good **team**.

You can help them
by solving the
Hidden Pictures
puzzles.

"Here is some felt!" says Nack.
"It does not look like a mouth.
Can we cut it with scissors?"

"Yes," says Nick.
"That is a great idea!"

Help Nick and Nack.
Find 5 pairs of scissors hidden in the picture.

Happy reading!

It is a snowy day.

Nick and Nack play outside.

They have fun in the snow.

But it is very cold.

"*Brrr,*" says Nick.

"Let's go inside," says Nack.

"Oh no!" says Nack. "I lost a mitten."

"Oh no!" says Nick. "I lost a sock."

They look in the pile of clothes.

No mitten. No sock.

Nick has just one sock.

Nack has just one mitten.

"What can we do with one sock and one mitten?" asks Nack.

"We can make puppets!" says Nick.

"How can we make puppets?"

asks Nack.

"First, our puppets need eyes," says Nick.

"What can we use to make eyes?" asks Nack.

"These balls are too big," says Nick.

"These beads are too small," says Nack.

"These eyes are just right," says Nick.

"They will move with my puppet!"

"Can I use buttons to make eyes?" asks Nack.

"Yes," says Nick.

"Buttons will make colorful eyes!"

Help Nick and Nack.

Find 5 buttons hidden in the picture.

"Next, our puppets need hair,"
says Nick.

"What can we use for hair?"
asks Nack.

"Let's use something soft,"
says Nick.

"I do not have hair," says Nack.
"But I can help find some!"

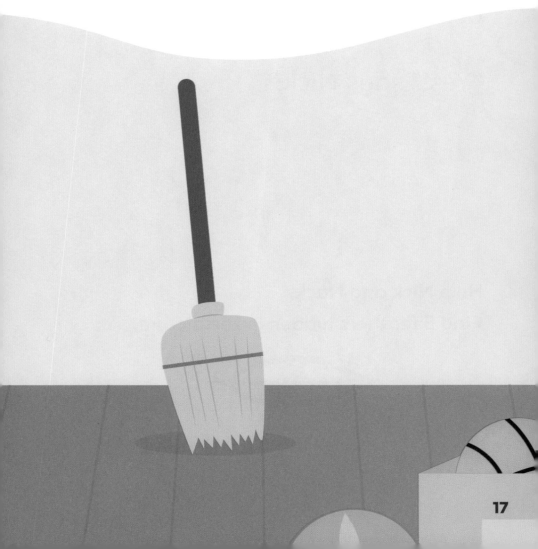

"I found yarn!" says Nack.

"We can use yarn to make hair," says Nick.

"Can we also use feathers?" asks Nack.

"Yes!" says Nick.

Help Nick and Nack.
Find 5 feathers hidden in the picture.

"Next, our puppets each need a mouth," says Nick. "We can use felt."

"I can help find felt," says Nack.

Nack finds a flag.

He finds a flower.

He finds a fan.

He cannot find felt.

"Here is some felt!" says Nack.

"It does not look like a mouth.

Can we cut it with scissors?"

"Yes," says Nick.

"That is a great idea!"

Help Nick and Nack.

Find 5 pairs of scissors hidden in the picture.

"Time to make our puppets!"
says Nick.

Nick puts eyes on his sock.

Nack puts eyes on his mitten.

Nick adds yarn for hair.

Nack adds feathers for hair.

Nick cuts out a mouth.

He puts it on.

"My puppet has a big smile,"

he says.

Nack cuts out a mouth.

He puts it on.

"My puppet has lots of teeth,"
he says.

"The puppets are done," says Nick.

"What can we do
with our puppets?" asks Nack.

"We can put on a puppet show!"
says Nick.

"That sounds like fun!" says Nack.

"Wait!" says Nick.

"Who will watch our puppet show?"

Help Nick and Nack.
Find 5 teddy bears hidden in the picture.

Make Your Own PUPPET!

WHAT YOU NEED:
- Sock or mitten
- Glue
- Wiggly eyes or buttons
- Yarn
- Marker
- Felt
- Scissors
- Ribbons

1
EYES
- Glue two wiggly eyes or buttons on top of the sock or mitten to make eyes.

2
HAIR
- Cut yarn as long as you wish.
- Glue yarn to the top of the puppet's head.

3 MOUTH

- Using a marker, draw a mouth on a piece of felt.
- Cut the mouth out.
- Glue the mouth onto the puppet.

This mouth is a semicircle, but you can make the mouth any shape you want!

4 ACCESSORIES

- Use ribbons and felt to create accessories for your puppet, such as clothing or hair accessories.

Nick and Nack's TIPS

- Gather your supplies before you start crafting.
- Ask an adult or robot for help with anything sharp or hot.
- Clean up your workspace when your craft is done.

For information about permission to reprint
selections from this book, please contact
permissions@highlights.com.

Published by Highlights Press
815 Church Street
Honesdale, Pennsylvania 18431
ISBN (paperback): 978-1-68437-933-0
ISBN (hardcover): 978-1-68437-985-9
ISBN (ebook): 978-1-64472-236-7

Library of Congress Control Number: 2020933674
Printed in Melrose Park, IL, USA
Mfg. 09/2020
First edition
Visit our website at Highlights.com.
10 9 8 7 6 5 4 3 2 1

Craft instructions by Elizabeth Wyrsch-Ba
Craft sample and photos by Lisa Glover

LEXILE®, LEXILE FRAMEWORK® ,
LEXILE ANALYZER®, the LEXILE®
logo and POWERV® are trademarks of
MetaMetrics, Inc., and are registered
in the United States and abroad. The
trademarks and names of other companies and
products mentioned herein are the property of their
respective owners. Copyright © 2019 MetaMetrics,
Inc. All rights reserved.

For assistance in the preparation of this book,
the editors would like to thank Vanessa Maldonado,
MSEd, MS Literacy Ed. K–12, Reading/LA Consultant
Cert., K–5 Literacy Instructional Coach; and
Gina Shaw.